GRISELDA F.G.M.'S SILVER BIRTHDAY

Griselda the fairy-godmother is back! As usual she is busy trying to help out her friends with her loopy spells. But Griselda is so busy helping everybody else, she doesn't have time to prepare for her own birthday party . . .

Margaret Ryan's humorous stories about Fat Witch and King Tubbitum have made her a popular author with younger readers. She has written two other books for Blackie, *Griselda F.G.M.* (to which this is a follow-up) and *The Saturday Knight*. Margaret lives in Inverclyde.

By the same author

Griselda F.G.M.
The Saturday Knight

GRISELDA F.G.M.'S SILVER BIRTHDAY

Margaret Ryan

Illustrated by John Eastwood

BLACKIE CHILDREN'S BOOKS

BLACKIE CHILDREN'S BOOKS

Published by the Penguin Group
Penguin Books Ltd, 27 Wrights Lane, London W8 5TZ, England
Penguin Books USA Inc., 375 Hudson Street, New York, New York 10014, USA
Penguin Books Australia Ltd, Ringwood, Victoria, Australia
Penguin Books Canada Ltd, 10 Alcorn Avenue, Toronto, Ontario, Canada M4V 3B2
Penguin Books (NZ) Ltd, 182–190 Wairau Road, Auckland 10, New Zealand

Penguin Books Ltd, Registered Offices: Harmondsworth, Middlesex, England

First published 1993
10 9 8 7 6 5 4 3 2 1
First edition

Text copyright © Margaret Ryan, 1993
Illustrations copyright © John Eastwood, 1993

The moral right of the author has been asserted

Filmset in 14/17pt Linotype Plantin
by Rowland Phototypesetting Ltd
Bury St Edmunds, Suffolk
Made and printed in Great Britain by
Butler & Tanner Ltd, Frome and London

A CIP catalogue record for this book is available from the British Library

ISBN 0–216–94000–1

1 Griselda F.G.M. and the Silver Birthday

It was nearly Griselda the fairy-godmother's silver birthday, and she was planning a party. She sat by the fire in her cottage, writing out her party invitations.

'I hope everyone can come,' she said to Samuel, her multi-coloured mouse. 'When I've finished writing out these invitations will you help me post them?'

Samuel snored loudly in reply. He was curled up inside one of Griselda's old socks, dreaming of a mouse birthday with lots of presents of smelly cheese.

Just then the alarm on Griselda's

micro-chipped and scratched super fairy-godmother watch went BLEEP BLEEP.

'Ah,' she said, putting down her pen. 'Time to look through the magic window and see who needs my help today.'

Samuel immediately wakened up, and leapt out of the old sock. He liked looking through the magic window. He ran up Griselda's arm and on to her shoulder.

Griselda went over to the cottage window. It was divided into six panes of glass, five clear and one cloudy. Griselda blew gently on the cloudy one, then rubbed it with her sleeve. Slowly a picture began to appear . . .

'Why, it's Duchess Dotty,' she said. 'I wonder why she needs my help today?'

Duchess Dotty was sitting in the middle of a pile of old family portraits, trying to clean them.

'My ancestors were a horrible-looking lot,' she said. 'Just look at the size of great-aunt Ermintrude's feet, and I'm sure that's a drip on the end of great-great uncle Fred's nose. Wish I'd never taken him down now to wipe it. How am I going to get all these portraits cleaned and put back up on the walls before the tourists get

here? And I've lost great-grandfather George somewhere. I'm certain he was lying around here a minute ago.'

'Oh dear, dear,' said Griselda, sucking in her cheeks and shaking her head. 'I think I'd better whizz off, and give Duchess Dotty a hand. Are you coming, Samuel?'

Samuel blew out his cheeks and nodded his head. 'I suppose I'd better come and make sure you don't go dotty,' he said.

Then he grabbed a strand of Griselda's long fair hair, swung on the end of it, and plopped into the pocket of her T-shirt. The pocket was the safest place to be when whizzing about with Griselda.

While Samuel held on tight, and prepared himself for take-off, Griselda did a little disco dance on the carpet, then said the magic words: TIME TO BE OFF TO

THE STATELY HOME. And they were off,
whizzing through the air with a *WHISH*, a
WHOOSH and a *WHIRL*.

And before you could say PLEASE
WIPE YOUR FEET, they had landed in the
stately home, in the middle of the great
hall, in the middle of the portrait of great-
grandfather George.

'Oops, sorry everyone,' said Griselda,
trying to wipe her footprints off

great-grandfather George's beard. 'I'm not very good at landings.'

'About as good as a fairy gorilla,' muttered Samuel. But Duchess Dotty was delighted to see them.

'Yoo-hoo, Griselda. Yoo-hoo, Samuel,' she said. 'Have you come to look round the stately home? It is in a bit of a state, I'm afraid. I don't know how I'm going to get these portraits cleaned and hung back up before the tourists get here. I wanted to hang them up quite high too, so that they didn't frighten the children.'

'I see what you mean,' said Samuel, diving back into Griselda's T-shirt pocket. 'They are incredibly ugly, aren't they? No offence, Duchess.'

'We've come to lend a hand with them,' said Griselda. 'I'm sure I know a spell that will have them cleaned and hung back up in no time.'

And before anyone could stop her, she did a little disco dance on the stone floor and said the magic words:

ROSES ARE RED
VIOLETS ARE BLUE
BROWN STRING AND SEALING WAX
HANG PORTRAITS NEW.

There was a *FIZZ*, a *THUMP* and a *BANG*, and all the dirt disappeared from the portraits and they flew straight up and stuck themselves to the ceiling.

'Oh dear,' said Griselda, 'I don't think that spell's quite right somehow.'

Just then a large coach drew up outside.

'Oh no,' said Duchess Dotty. 'The tourists have arrived.'

'Don't worry, Duchess,' said Griselda. 'You go and let them in. I have an idea.'

Then she said to Samuel, 'Lie down on the floor and gaze up at the ceiling as though you were admiring the portraits.'

'But they're horrible,' said Samuel.

'They don't look so bad from here,' said Griselda. 'Shush, here come the tourists.'

'And this is the great hall,' Duchess Dotty was explaining to them. 'And these are the portraits of my ancestors . . . ahem

. . . up on the ceiling.' Then she looked at Griselda and Samuel lying on the floor gazing admiringly upwards. 'You have to lie on the floor to look at them properly.'

'Great idea,' said the tourists. 'That way we can have a rest. Our feet are killing us.'

Griselda beamed and nudged Samuel. 'Great idea, Samuel,' she said. 'Did you hear that?'

But Samuel was too busy snoring to notice.

And Griselda was so pleased at how well everything had worked out that when they got back to the cottage she stopped at the garden gate and said to Samuel, 'I think I'll put some photographs of you and me out on the mantelpiece. Perhaps the party guests would like to have a look at them. What do you think?'

'I think they'll think I'm incredibly handsome,' said Samuel.

2 Griselda and the Greengrocer

Griselda, the fairy-godmother, was standing on a wobbly stool trying to pin up some silver tinsel round the cottage walls.

'Oh dear, I'll never get everything ready in time for the party,' she said to Samuel, her multi-coloured mouse. 'Every time I

pin up this tinsel it falls back down again. Do you think I should try gluing it up instead?'

Samuel snored and whistled in reply. He was curled up inside the Christmas decoration box, sleeping peacefully on a snowy white Santa beard.

Just then the alarm on Griselda's micro-chipped and scratched super fairy-godmother watch went OINK OINK. Griselda waggled it in the air till it went BLEEP BLEEP.

'Ah,' she said, dropping the tinsel. 'Time to look through the magic window, and see who needs my help today.'

Samuel immediately wakened up and leapt out of the box. He liked looking through the magic window. He ran up Griselda's arm and on to her shoulder.

Griselda went over to the cottage window. It was divided into six panes of glass, five clear and one cloudy. Griselda blew gently on the cloudy one, then rubbed it with her sleeve. Slowly a picture began to appear . . .

'Why, it's Mr McMarrow, the green-grocer,' she said. 'I wonder why he needs my help today?'

Mr McMarrow was running round and round his shop, chasing a large black and white cat.

'Get out of here this minute, you mischievous moggy,' he shouted. 'Look what you've done. Business was bad enough without you upsetting all the fruit. Just look at the apples and pears scattered all over the floor, and my very best oranges rolling down the street. What a mess.'

'Oh dear, dear,' said Griselda, sucking in her cheeks and shaking her head. 'I think I'd better whizz off and give Mr McMarrow a hand. Are you coming, Samuel?'

Samuel blew out his cheeks and nodded his head. 'I suppose I'd better come and chase away that cat. Cats are afraid of mice, you know.'

Then he grabbed a strand of Griselda's long fair hair, swung on the end of it, and plopped into the pocket of her T-shirt. The pocket was the safest place to be when

whizzing about with Griselda.

While Samuel held on tight and prepared himself for take-off, Griselda did a little disco dance on the carpet, then said the magic words: TIME TO BE OFF TO THE GREENGROCER'S. And they were off, with a *WHISH*, a *WHOOSH* and a *WHIRL*.

And before you could say SIX ROSY APPLES they had landed in the greengrocer's, in the middle of the shop, in the middle of a large box of green grapes.

'Oops, sorry everyone,' said Griselda, trampling the grapes with her trainers. 'I'm not very good at landings.'

'About as good as a turkey on a trampoline,' muttered Samuel.

'Oh, it's you, Griselda,' groaned Mr McMarrow. 'That's all I need. First that cat tries to make my oranges into

marmalade, now you're trying to make my grapes into wine. What next?'

'I could make these plums disappear into my tum,' said Samuel.

'We just came to help,' said Griselda. 'I'm sure I know a spell that will put all the fruit back.'

And before anyone could stop her, she did a little disco dance on the shop floor and said the magic words:

ROSES ARE RED

VIOLETS ARE BLUE

PUT BACK THE FRUIT

AS GOOD AS NEW.

There was a *FIZZ*, a *THUMP* and a *BANG*, and all the apples and pears flew up from the shop floor, and all the oranges flew back through the shop door.

ZONK, a large orange bounced off Mr McMarrow's bald head.

ZAP, a red apple bounced off Griselda's left ear.

ZOOP, a green pear bounced off Samuel's black nose.

Then all the fruit was back in the boxes. All mixed up.

'Oh dear,' said Griselda, rubbing her ear. 'I don't think that spell's quite right somehow.'

Just then some customers came into the shop.

'Oh no,' said Mr McMarrow. 'What will they think of all this muddled-up fruit?'

'Don't worry, Mr McMarrow,' said Griselda. 'I'll serve the customers. I have an idea.'

'Hullo everyone,' she said to the customers. 'Have you heard about our special offer already? This week's star buy. Bags of mixed fruit to make jam.'

'Home-made jam,' said one customer.

'Oh, how lovely. I haven't had that for ages. I'll take six bags, please.'

'Home-made jam,' said another. 'What a great idea. I love it on hot scones. I'll have six bags too.'

Word of the special offer spread like jam on hot scones, and soon all Mr McMarrow's fruit was sold out.

'Griselda,' he said, 'I'm so sorry I was cross with you. You really are a marvel.'

Griselda beamed and nudged Samuel. 'A marvel, Samuel. Did you hear that?'

But Samuel was far too sleepy to notice. It's hard to stay awake with your tum full of plum.

And Griselda was so pleased at how well everything had turned out that when they got back to the cottage she stopped at the garden gate and said to Samuel, 'Perhaps I shouldn't worry about the silver tinsel falling down. You could help me hang up these new silver balls I've bought instead. What do you think?'

'Great idea,' said Samuel, admiring his reflection in the silver balls. 'That way there will be lots of little Samuels sparkling all round the room. Good thing I'm so incredibly handsome.'

3 Griselda and the Lollipop Lady

Griselda, the fairy-godmother, was examining her old jeans and T-shirt in a long mirror.

'Oh dear, these clothes don't look quite right for a party,' she said to Samuel, her multi-coloured mouse. 'I wonder if I'll have time to buy some new ones before my silver birthday. I can't really go dressed in these, can I?'

Samuel snored, whistled and squeaked in reply. He was curled up inside a knitted tea-cosy, dreaming of afternoon teas with chocolate éclairs and gooey meringues.

Just then the alarm on Griselda's

micro-chipped and scratched super fairy-godmother watch went PAMP PAMP. Griselda jiggled it up and down till it went BLEEP BLEEP.

'Ah,' she said, turning away from the mirror. 'Time to look through the magic window, and see who needs my help today.'

Samuel immediately wakened up, and leapt out of the tea-cosy. He liked looking through the magic window. He ran up Griselda's arm and on to her shoulder.

Griselda went over to the cottage window. It was divided into six panes of glass, five clear and one cloudy. Griselda blew gently on the cloudy one, then rubbed it with her sleeve. Slowly a picture began to appear . . .

'Why, it's Mrs Stravinsky, the lollipop lady,' she said. 'I wonder why she needs my help today?'

Mrs Stravinsky was standing by the kerb, her lollipop in one hand, and a huge hanky in the other.

'ATISHOO,' she sneezed. 'A-A-A-TISHOOOOO. Oh my goodness, the pensioners will catch this terrible cold when I take them across the road to their lunch club today. I really should go home to bed, but it's old Mrs Gordon's birthday, and her turn to help me carry the lollipop. What am I going to do? ATISHOO.'

'Oh dear, dear,' said Griselda, sucking in her cheeks and shaking her head. 'I think I'd better whizz off and give Mrs Stravinsky a hand. Are you coming, Samuel?'

Samuel blew out his cheeks and nodded his head. 'I love lollipops,' he said.

Then he grabbed a strand of Griselda's long fair hair, swung on the end of it, and plopped into the pocket of her T-shirt. The pocket was the safest place to be when whizzing about with Griselda.

While Samuel held on tight, and prepared himself for take-off, Griselda did a little disco dance on the carpet, then said the magic words: TIME TO BE OFF TO THE HIGH STREET. And they were off, with a *WHISH*, a *WHOOSH* and a *WHIRL*.

And before you could say STOP AT THE KERB they had landed in the High Street, in the middle of the pavement, in the middle of an enormous puddle.

'Oops, sorry everyone,' said Griselda, trying to shake her jeans and her trainers dry. 'I'm not very good at landings.'

'Good thing mice are waterproof,' muttered Samuel.

But Mrs Stravinsky was delighted to see them.

'Atishoo, Griselda. Atishoo, Samuel,' she said. 'It's lovely to see you, but don't come too close. You don't want to catch my cold. Would you like me to help you across the road?'

'No, no, it's you we've come to help, Mrs Stravinsky,' said Griselda. 'We'll take charge of the lollipop and see to old Mrs Gordon and the pensioners. You go off home. I know a spell that will take you there right away.'

And before anyone could stop her, she did a little disco dance on the pavement and said the magic words:

> ROSES ARE RED
> NOSES ARE TOO
> TAKE HOME MRS STRAVINSKY
> IN CASE SHE'S GOT FLU.

There was a *FIZZ*, a *THUMP* and a *BANG*, and Mrs Stravinsky disappeared off home. But the sneeze didn't. It went up and down the pavement, sneezing. ATISHOO, ATISHOO, ATISHOO.

'Bless you,' said Samuel.

'Oh dear,' said Griselda. 'I don't think that spell's quite right somehow.'

At that moment the pensioners arrived, and old Mrs Gordon said to Griselda, 'It's my birthday today. Can I help you carry the lollipop?'

'Certainly,' beamed Griselda. 'I hope

you don't find it too heavy with Samuel
sitting on the top.'

Then the rest of the pensioners said,
'Can we all have a shot at carrying your
lollipop, Griselda?'

'Is it everybody's birthday?'

'Might be,' said the pensioners. 'We're so old we've forgotten.'

Griselda stopped the traffic, and let all the pensioners have a shot at carrying the lollipop across the road. It took a long time.

HONK HONK, PEEP PEEP, HOOT HOOT.

The cars and lorries were getting fed up waiting.

'Time for another quick spell,' said Griselda.

'Oh no,' said Samuel.

But this one worked. A very quick disco dance, then . . .

ROSES ARE RED
VIOLETS ARE BLUE
MOVE ON THE PENSIONERS
THEY'RE CAUSING A QUEUE.

And all of a sudden the pensioners were speeded up and they crossed the road in double quick time.

'Whee-hee,' they yelled. 'Just look at us go. Griselda, you're wonderful.'

Then all the traffic got started again.

Griselda beamed and nudged Samuel. 'I'm wonderful,' she said. 'Did you hear that?'

But Samuel was too busy waving to the pensioners to notice.

And Griselda was so pleased at how well her *TWO* spells had worked out, that when they got back to the cottage she stopped at the garden gate and said to Samuel, 'I've been thinking, since my spells have been working out better, perhaps I could magic myself up a new fairy-godmother outfit for the party. What do you think?'

Samuel shook his head. 'Last time you tried that you got a ghastly pink frock and a silver wand. I'm an incredibly handsome mouse, and I'm not going out with you wearing that.'

4   Griselda and the Beansprouts

Griselda, the fairy-godmother, was sitting at the kitchen table trying to blow up a pile of silver balloons for the party.

'I'll never get all these blown up in time,' she puffed. 'It's jolly hard work, but I love having balloons at a party, don't you, Samuel?'

Samuel, her multi-coloured mouse, snored, whistled, squeaked and burbled in reply. He was curled up inside the washing-basket, dreaming of golden crumpets dripping with runny honey.

Just then, the alarm on Griselda's micro-chipped and scratched super fairy-godmother watch went WHIRR WHIRR. Griselda gave it a good thump till it went BLEEP BLEEP.

'Ah,' she said, putting down the balloons. 'Time to look through the magic window, and see who needs my help today.'

Samuel immediately wakened up, and leapt out of the washing-basket. He liked looking through the magic window. He ran up Griselda's arm and on to her shoulder.

Griselda went over to the cottage window. It was divided into six panes of glass, five clear and one cloudy. Griselda blew gently on the cloudy one, then rubbed it with her sleeve. Slowly a picture began to appear . . .

'Why, it's little Lee Ho,' she said. 'I wonder why he needs my help today?'

Little Lee Ho was sitting in the kitchen of his father's Chinese restaurant, looking at some very tiny beansprouts.

'Just look at the size of these beansprouts,' he said. 'How am I going to grow up to be a famous chef like my dad and my grandad if I can't even grow beansprouts? Grandad is coming to have his lunch at the restaurant today, and I promised he could taste some of my beansprouts.'

'Oh dear, dear,' said Griselda, sucking in her cheeks and shaking her head. 'I think I'd better whizz off and give little Lee Ho a hand. Are you coming, Samuel?'

Samuel blew out his cheeks and nodded his head. 'You bet,' he said. 'I've never tasted beansprouts.'

Then he grabbed a strand of Griselda's long fair hair, swung on the end of it, and plopped into the pocket of her T-shirt. The pocket was the safest place to be when whizzing about with Griselda.

While Samuel held on tight and prepared for take-off, Griselda did a little disco dance on the carpet, then said the magic words: TIME TO BE OFF TO THE CHINESE RESTAURANT. And they were off, whizzing through the air with a *WHISH*, a *WHOOSH* and a *WHIRL*.

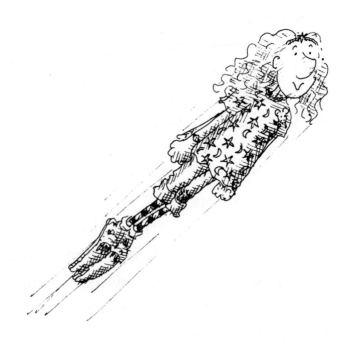

And before you could say CHICKEN
FRIED RICE, they had landed in the
Chinese restaurant, in the middle of the
kitchen, in the middle of the pots and
pans.

'Oops, sorry everyone,' said Griselda,
clattering her way through them. 'I'm not
very good at landings.'

'Perhaps you should wear a parachute,'

43

muttered Samuel.

But little Lee Ho was delighted to see them.

'Hullo, Griselda. Hullo, Samuel,' he said. 'Have you come for lunch? Grandad is coming to try some of my beansprouts for lunch today, but I think he'll go hungry.'

'Don't worry, Lee Ho,' said Griselda. 'We've come to lend a hand. I'm sure I know a spell that will make the beansprouts grow.'

And before anyone could stop her, she did a little disco dance on the tiled floor, and said the magic words:

ROSES ARE RED
VIOLETS ARE BLUE
COME ON BEANSPROUTS GROW
UP AND UP, DO.

There was a *FIZZ*, a *THUMP* and a *BANG*, and the beansprouts started to grow and grow and grow. Soon the kitchen was covered in a forest of beansprouts.

'Help,' yelled Samuel. 'I'm lost in the forest. I may have to eat my way out.'

'Oh dear,' said Griselda. 'I don't think that spell's quite right somehow.'

At that moment a long red car drew up outside.

'Oh no,' said Lee Ho. 'Grandad.'

'Don't worry, Lee Ho,' said Griselda. 'You go and let him in. I have an idea.'

She quickly found some paper and a pen and wrote out a big notice. She pinned the notice up on the door of the kitchen. It said: BEANSPROUTS FOR SALE. PICK YOUR OWN.

When Grandad came in with Lee Ho he was amazed.

'Good gracious,' he said. 'I've never seen beansprouts like these before. Can I have some for my lunch?'

'Just pick your own, Grandad,' said Griselda, winking at Lee Ho. 'The restaurant is self-service today.'

Little Lee Ho winked back. 'Thanks, Griselda,' he whispered. 'You're a genius.'

Griselda beamed and nudged Samuel. 'I'm a genius, Samuel. Did you hear that?'

But Samuel was too busy munching beansprouts to notice.

And Griselda was so pleased at how well everything had turned out that when they got back to the cottage she stopped at the garden gate and said to Samuel, 'Those beansprouts have given me an idea for the party. Once I get all the silver balloons blown up, I could put long strings on them and have them sprouting from the bushes in the garden. What do you think?'

'I think that would be a good idea,' said Samuel. 'Then I could come along with my incredibly handsome claws and burst them.'

POP, POP, POP . . .

5 Griselda and the District Nurse

Griselda, the fairy-godmother, was up to her elbows in flour trying to make fairy-godmother cakes for the party.

'I hope these cakes turn out all right,' she said to Samuel, her multi-coloured mouse. 'I'm not too sure how long they should be in the oven. Once they're ready, will you help me ice them?'

Samuel snored, whistled, squeaked, burbled and burped in reply. He was curled up inside an empty chocolate cookie box, dreaming of eating another box of chocolate cookies.

Just then the alarm on Griselda's

micro-chipped and scratched super fairy-godmother watch went GOOD MORNING SLEEPY-HEADS. Griselda wiggled it till it went BLEEP BLEEP.

'Ah,' she said, wiping her floury hands on her jeans. 'Time to look through the magic window and see who needs my help today.'

Samuel immediately wakened up. He liked looking through the magic window. He ran up Griselda's arm and on to her shoulder.

Griselda went over to the cottage window. It was divided into six panes of glass, five clear and one cloudy. Griselda blew gently on the cloudy one, then rubbed it with her sleeve. Slowly a picture began to appear . . .

'Why, it's Nurse Nightingale,' she said. 'I wonder why she needs my help today?'

Nurse Nightingale was standing on the edge of the pavement with her head stuck under the bonnet of her little blue Mini.

'Bothersome bandages,' she said. 'Why won't this old car start? It's got plenty of petrol in its tank, plenty of water in its radiator and plenty of air in its tyres. I'd better get out my tool-kit and see what I can do, but I really don't have time to fiddle about. I've got patients to see.'

'Oh dear, dear,' said Griselda, sucking in her cheeks and shaking her head. 'I think I'd better whizz off and give Nurse Nightingale a hand. Are you coming, Samuel?'

Samuel blew out his cheeks and nodded his head. 'Nurse Nightingale keeps jelly babies in her bag for good little mice,' he said.

Then he grabbed a strand of Griselda's long fair hair, swung on the end of it, and plopped into the pocket of her T-shirt. The pocket was the safest place to be when whizzing about with Griselda.

While Samuel held on tight, Griselda did a little disco dance on the carpet, then said the magic words: TIME TO BE OFF TO NURSE NIGHTINGALE. And they were off with a *WHISH*, a *WHOOSH* and a *WHIRL*.

And before you could say HORRIBLE HEADACHES, they had landed beside Nurse Nightingale, in the middle of the pavement, in the middle of her tool-kit.

'Oops, sorry everyone,' said Griselda, scattering spanners and screwdrivers everywhere. 'I'm not very good at landings.'

'You've put a real spanner in the works this time,' muttered Samuel, rescuing one from the engine.

But Nurse Nightingale was delighted to see them.

'Hi there, Griselda. Give me five, mouse,' she said. 'I hope you don't want a lift anywhere. Looks like this old car's going nowhere.'

'I've never been to nowhere,' said Samuel.

'We've come to lend a hand with your car,' said Griselda. 'I'm sure I know a spell

that will get it going in no time.'

And before anyone could stop her, she

did a little disco dance on the pavement and said the magic words:

ROSES ARE RED
VIOLETS ARE BLUE
PLEASE MAKE THIS CAR
JUST LIKE BRAND-NEW.

There was a *FIZZ*, a *THUMP* and a *BANG*, and the bonnet of the Mini thudded shut, the engine roared to life, and the car drove off by itself.

'Oh no,' said Nurse Nightingale. 'Now where is it going?'

'Nowhere?' said Samuel.

'Oh dear,' said Griselda. 'I don't think that spell's quite right somehow, but don't worry, I have another idea. How would you like to be District Flying Nurse Nightingale?'

'I'd love it,' said Nurse Nightingale.

'Better hang on to Griselda's hand then,' said Samuel. 'You're too big to fit in her T-shirt pocket.'

Then Griselda said the magic words: TIME TO BE OFF TO SEE THE PATIENTS. And they were off with a *WHISH*, a

WHOOSH and a *WHIRL*.

And the patients were so pleased to see them, they didn't mind that they landed right in beside them, in the middle of the bed, in the middle of their tea and cakes.

'Griselda, you're a tonic,' they said. 'We feel better already.'

Griselda beamed and nudged Samuel. 'I'm a tonic,' she said. 'Did you hear that?'

But Samuel was asleep on the duvet, too full up with tea and cakes to notice.

And Griselda was so pleased at how well everything had worked out, that when they got back to the cottage she stopped at the garden gate and said to Samuel, 'Perhaps we could take some of my fairy-godmother cakes to the patients whose cakes we squashed. What do you think?'

'I think I might try baking incredibly handsome mouse cakes,' said Samuel.

6   Griselda and the Postman

It was the morning of the silver birthday party, and Griselda, the fairy-godmother, was up very early trying to get everything ready.

'Oh dear,' she said to Samuel, her multi-coloured mouse. 'Nothing seems to be working out right for this party. All the silver decorations are falling down, the fairy-godmother cakes are a disaster, and I haven't had time to buy myself anything new to wear. What am I going to do?'

Samuel snored, whistled, squeaked, burbled, burped and snuffled in reply. He was still in his pyjamas in his little mouse bed. It was far too early for him to be awake.

Just then the alarm on Griselda's micro-chipped and scratched super fairy-godmother watch went THIS IS YOUR EARLY MORNING ALARM CALL. Griselda gave it a really good thump till it went BLEEP BLEEP.

'Ah,' said Griselda, forgetting to worry about the party for a moment. 'Time to look through the magic window and see who needs my help today.'

Samuel immediately wakened up. He liked looking through the magic window. He ran up Griselda's arm and on to her shoulder.

Griselda went over to the cottage win-dow. It was divided into six panes of glass, five clear and one cloudy. Griselda blew gently on the cloudy one, then rubbed it with her sleeve. Slowly a picture began to appear . . .

'Why, it's Postman Brown,' she said. 'I wonder why he needs my help today?'

Postman Brown was standing inside the post office, puffing and panting as he tried to heave his postman's sack on to his shoulder.

'Gracious me,' he said, 'either I'm getting too old for this job or this sack is extra heavy today. I can hardly lift it. I'll never get my round finished in time to go to Griselda's party.'

'Oh dear, dear,' said Griselda, sucking in her cheeks and shaking her head. 'I think I'd better whizz off and give Postman Brown a hand. Are you coming, Samuel?'

Samuel blew out his cheeks and nodded his head.

'I could be a post mouse,' he said.

Then he grabbed a strand of Griselda's long fair hair, swung on the end of it, and plopped into the pocket of her T-shirt. The pocket was the safest place to be when whizzing about with Griselda.

While Samuel held on tight, Griselda did a little disco dance on the carpet, then

said the magic words: TIME TO BE OFF
TO POSTMAN BROWN. And they were off
with a *WHISH*, a *WHOOSH* and a
WHIRL.

And before you could say FIRST CLASS
STAMP, they had landed beside Postman

Brown, in the middle of the post office, in the middle of all the sacks of letters.

'Oops, sorry everyone,' said Griselda, tripping over the sacks. 'I'm not very good at landings.'

'I suppose it's lucky we didn't land inside a pillar-box,' muttered Samuel.

But Postman Brown was delighted to see them.

'Hullo, Griselda. Hullo, little Samuel,' he said. 'You're up early today. Are you all ready for the party?'

'No,' said Samuel.

'Well . . . not really ready exactly,' said Griselda.

Postman Brown laughed. 'Well, I won't be ready either till I get all these letters delivered. It's going to take me ages today.'

'That's why we've come to lend a hand,'

said Griselda. 'We don't want you missing the party. I'm sure I know a spell . . . '

But before she could go on Postman Brown stopped her.

'I'm sure you do, Griselda,' he said. 'But we can't use a spell to deliver the mail. Post Office regulations, you see.'

'Oh dear,' said Griselda. 'How can we help you then?'

'Why don't you deliver half the letters in my sack and I'll deliver the other half? That way we'll be finished twice as fast, and I'll get to your silver birthday party in good time.'

'All right,' said Griselda. 'It shouldn't take too long.'

But it did. They had to walk down a lot of long streets, they had to climb up a lot of steep stairs, and they had to be careful not to nip their fingers and claws in a lot of snappy letter-boxes.

'I don't think I want to be a post mouse after all,' said Samuel. 'Delivering letters is really hard work.'

'And it's getting really late,' said Griselda when they'd finally finished. 'We must hurry home and get everything ready for the party.'

But when they got back to the cottage Griselda stopped at the garden gate in amazement. The garden was full of silver balloons, and the cottage was covered in silver tinsel.

'Oh look, Samuel,' said Griselda. 'Who could have done all this?'

'Dunno,' said Samuel. 'Maybe YOU'VE got a fairy-godmother.' Then the cottage door opened and all Griselda's friends said, 'Welcome to your silver birthday party, Griselda. We knew you were too busy helping us to have much time to prepare for it, so we came to help you for a change.'

'Oh my goodness,' said Griselda as she

looked around. There were beautiful silver decorations everywhere.

'I did the decorations,' said Mr McMarrow the greengrocer.

The table was laid with a superb birthday feast.

'Grandad and I did the cooking,' said little Lee Ho.

In the middle of the feast was an enormous birthday cake.

'I made the cake,' said Nurse Nightingale.

On the fireside chair were some birthday presents.

'New jeans,' said Griselda, 'with a silver buckle on the belt, a new T-shirt with silver stars and shiny silver trainers. Oh, my!'

'Has the T-shirt got a pocket?' asked Samuel.

'Oh, yes,' laughed Mrs Stravinsky. 'I made sure of that.'

'And I brought you this,' said Duchess Dotty. 'It's a fairy-godmother ancestor portrait to hang up on your wall.'

'Oh no, she's wearing one of those ghastly pink frocks and carrying a silver wand,' said Samuel. 'And she's incredibly

74

ugly. No offence, Duchess.'

Griselda gave him a nudge to be quiet. 'It's lovely, Duchess Dotty,' she said. 'My very own ancestor. Thank you very much.'

'And this lollipop in the silver paper is from me,' said Samuel. 'I only licked it a little bit to see that it was all right.'

Then Postman Brown brought out his big sack. 'All the letters I delivered were birthday cards for you, Griselda. While you delivered the others I sneaked back here to help get things ready for the party.'

'Thank you all so much,' said Griselda. 'Everything is just lovely. I don't know what to say.'

'I do,' said Samuel. 'We all think you're wonderful, a marvel, a tonic, a genius and you get great ideas. Happy silver birthday, Griselda.'

Story Factory titles